when will we play again?

STORY BY
DARIEN HEAP, M.D.

ILLUSTRATIONS BY
COREY D. MACOUREK

ISBN: 978-1-7168-4157-6 (sc)
ISBN: 978-1-7168-4158-3 (hc)
ISBN: 978-1-7168-4156-9 (e)

Lulu Publishing Services rev. date: 06/27/2020

Dedication

This book is dedicated to my son, *Kiren*,
and all the other preschool children that are struggling
to make sense of the new world in which they live
with the coronavirus.

Acknowledgements

This book would not have been possible without the tireless support
of *Hussain Chinoy, Eric Lopresti*, and its illustrator, *Corey Macourek*,
all of whom have my deepest gratitude. Additional thanks belong to
John Fox, Crystal & Dexter, and my wife, *Gita*, who has been on the
front lines caring for patients with COVID-19.

Dad and I are looking at our travel album again.

I love doing this more and more lately.

I remember playing on the beach — there was such a large crab! Grandma came with us to my favorite theme park, and we had such fun!

"When can we go somewhere and play?"

"Soon. Maybe. Hopefully soon — once the coronavirus is gone."

We drove to the nursing home
where Grandma lives.

We're no longer allowed to go in,
and I really miss Grandma's hugs.

"Can Grandma come out and play?"

"Look, we're playing right now! See?"

Grandma and I have a nice time making
funny faces at each other
through the fence.

After we say goodbye
to Grandma, we look for
something to do outdoors.

The park near the nursing
home is roped off.

"When will we be able to play?"

I can tell Dad wants to push me on the swing, I think he likes it more than me.

"I don't know," Dad said.

We walk around the park back towards the car to go home.

The park looks like it's not having fun, either.

Dad and I walk around the trailhead, but there's a sign he points to.

"National parks will be closed for a while."

"Not yet."

Kicking the ball around reminds me of my friends and the fun we had during matches.

"No. Probably not for a while." Dad said.

We pick up a few vegetables and some pasta.
There are a few empty spots in the store.

Following dinner preparations,
Dad says he needs to go to work,
but he hasn't left in the morning
to drive to the office in a long time.

Once we're done working,
we make more masks
to be safe outside.

"I'd rather be playing now."

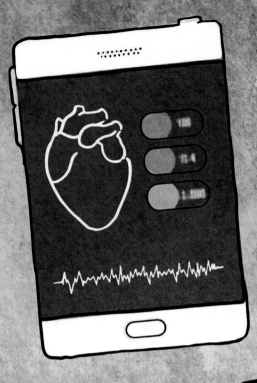

Dad sits me down
to tell me some news.

Grandma is sick and has been
moved to the hospital.

Because she's at the hospital,
we can't even visit her.
Not even over video.

Dad and I sit down
to have a family talk.

He sets dominoes down
a few inches apart.
When I push them over,
they don't hit the other ones,
and fewer dominoes fall down.

"How soon until we play again?"

"It's hard to say, Son."

I miss hugging Grandma.

But if being a little farther away
means fewer people get sick,
that sounds like a good idea.

"If the test says the right thing,
I suppose so," Dad said.

In addition to masks and being
a bit farther away from people,
Dad explains that testing will be an
activity everyone will do.

Finally he says that a vaccine will come and prevent us from ever worrying about the virus again.

It's a great day! We get a phone call that says Grandma has recovered and is back at the nursing home!

We rush off to video chat with her,
and she's so happy to see me.
I'm happy, too!

"Papa, when will we play again?"

Dad looks at me with a big smile and says...

"We can play now. Starting right now!"

We can play in the park, just in new and different ways.

We go to the park, and there are more people,
sharing our space together. We're all having fun!

The days ahead will be different, but together
we will enjoy ourselves and be safe.

With all our extra together time, our photo album is full of new pictures of Grandma and Papa and me.

Every new day is different,
and Papa and I love making
new memories
playing together!

The following pages are
left blank so that you can
create your own new hopeful
memories.

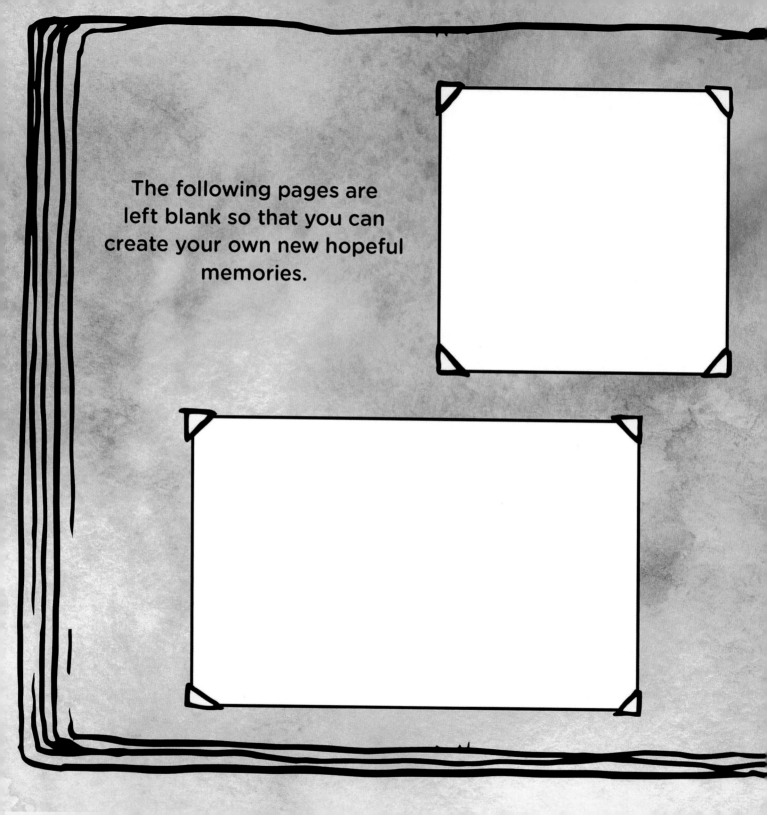

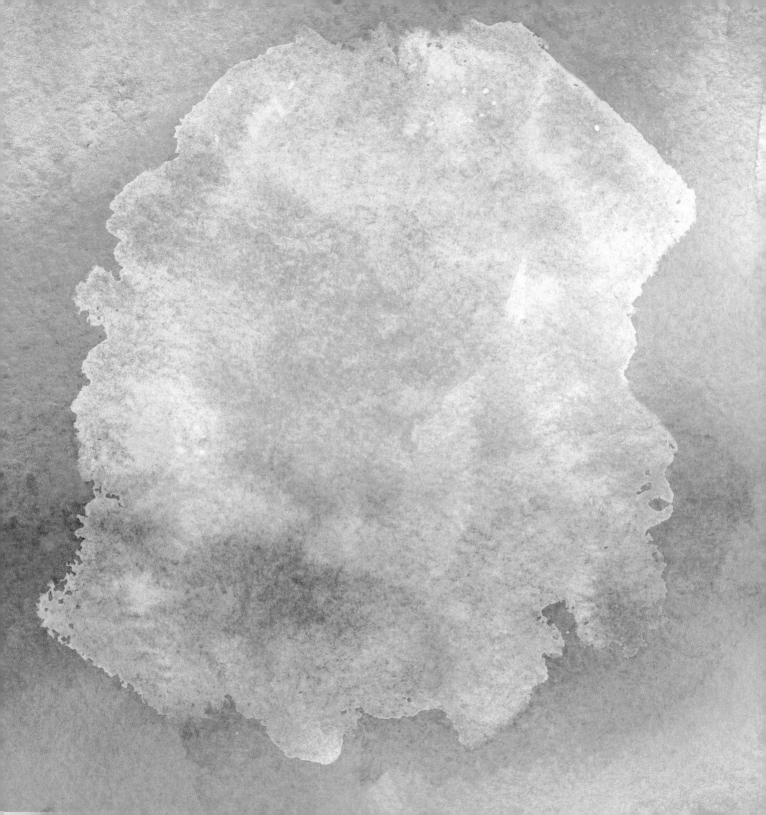

Corey Macourek is a full-time digital artist and animator with over 25 years of experience in award-winning multimedia creation.

He lives in Tacoma, WA with his cat and intergalactic action figure collection.

Dedicated to G, M, and health workers around the globe. Special thanks to Britton Sukys for his talented support.

Made in the USA
Coppell, TX
23 August 2020